No Fear, No Fear, Jesus is Here!

Text copyright © 2020 Andrea Whiston.

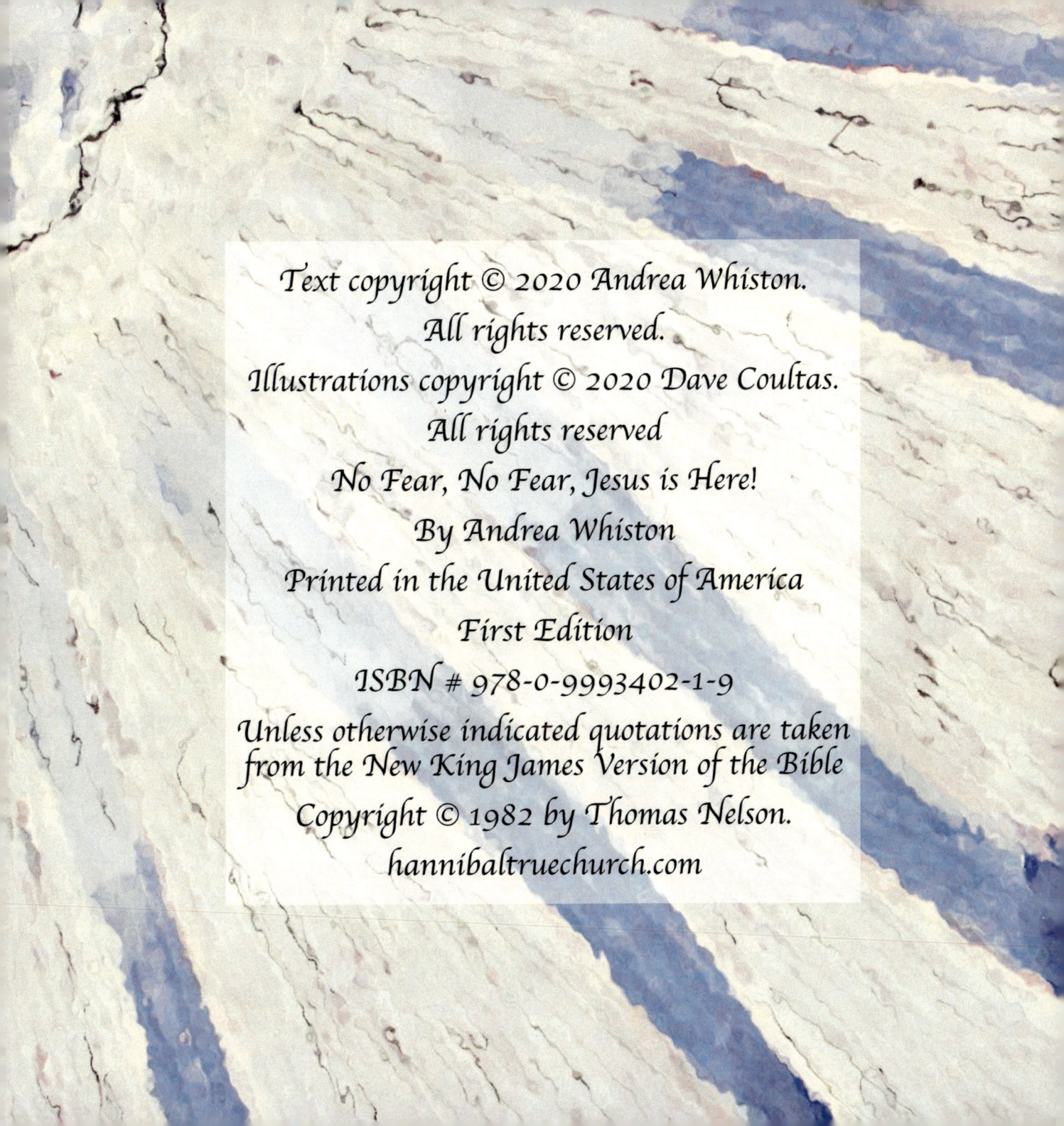

All rights reserved.

Illustrations copyright © 2020 Dave Coultas.

All rights reserved

No Fear, No Fear, Jesus is Here!

By Andrea Whiston

Printed in the United States of America

First Edition

ISBN # 978-0-9993402-1-9

Unless otherwise indicated quotations are taken from the New King James Version of the Bible

Copyright © 1982 by Thomas Nelson.

hannibaltruechurch.com

Introduction

I wrote this book to help children come out of their fears and to come to know Jesus is with them everywhere they go, even when they don't see Him. My nieces and nephews were always afraid to go downstairs to the basement by themselves, so I would always tell them that you're not going alone, Jesus is with you! I would tell them "No fear, Jesus is here." I would be in the other room and I would hear them going down to the basement saying, "No fear, Jesus is here." I have a nephew that is now four years old and right before he is going downstairs to the basement, he will look at me and say, "No fear, Jesus is here right?"

Isaiah 41:10

Have I not commanded you? Be strong and of good courage; do not be afraid, nor be dismayed, for the Lord your God is with you wherever you go."

The Lord had put it on my heart to write a children's book. All the characters in my book are portraying a family member. As I was writing this book, I asked my family members "If they could be an animal what would they be?" Deano the Eagle is my Brother in Christ Dean, Atarah the Tiger is my little Sister Kristen, Hot chocolate the Lioness is my Sister in Christ Marilyn, Thomas the Pig is my Step Father Tom, Abby the piglet is my Sister Abby, Terrance the Horse is my Mom Teri and Wellington the cow is my Nephew Avory.

No Fear, No Fear, Jesus is Here!
by Andrea Whiston
Illustrated by Dave Coultas

Deano the Eagle soaring high in the sky, far in the distance he heard a loud cry.

Deano the Eagle swooped down to see, there he saw Atarah the Tiger afraid as can be.

Atarah the Tiger said with a shout, "Help, help the spiders are out!"

Deano the Eagle smiled and said, "Trust in Jesus, and you shall be led."

Atarah the Tiger said, "What do you mean? How do I trust someone I have never seen?"

Deano the Eagle replied,

"Even though you don't see the Lord, He is there to lead you on forward. Just believe in your heart that He is near, saying out loud no fear, no fear, Jesus is here!"

Atarah the Tiger did what her friend had said and was able to move past the spiders ahead.

Deano the Eagle moved on by praising the Lord as he soared high.

Atarah the Tiger amazed by what Jesus has done was totally ready to have some fun.

Atarah the Tiger was excited to see Hot Chocolate the Lioness up in the tree. Hot Chocolate the Lioness said with a frown, "Help me I am afraid to get down."

Atarah the Tiger smiled and said, "Trust in Jesus and you shall be led."

Hot Chocolate the Lioness said, "What do you mean? How can I trust someone I have never seen?"

Atarah the Tiger answered, "Even though you don't see the Lord,
He is there to lead you on forward.
Just believe in your heart that He is near, saying out loud no fear,
no fear, Jesus is here!"

Hot Chocolate the Lioness said, "What a silly thing to say, I can't get out of the tree that way!"

Atarah the Tiger said, "I was afraid of spiders and He helped me. Jesus will be there for you, just trust Him and you will see."

Hot Chocolate the Lioness decided to give it a try, with a big leap jumped right into the pigsty.

Abby the Piglet surprised by the splash, made a loud squeal and ran in a flash.

Thomas the Pig all covered in mud, said with a grin "What was that thud?"

Hot Chocolate the Lioness was happy as can be

saying to her friends,

"It is just me!"

Thomas the Pig was very glad to see
his friend made it down safely.
Abby the Piglet came back in a flash, seeing it was
Hot Chocolate the Lioness who made the splash.

Terrance the Horse heard all the chattering, ran over to where they were all gathering.

Terrance the Horse said with a Nay, "What is going on over here today?"

Abby the Piglet was excited to share that she learned there is nothing to fear.

As they were all talking about their day, they heard something over by the hay.

They all ran to see what it could be, it was Wellington the Cow scared intensely.

Terrance the Horse said, "What do you fear?" Wellington the Cow said, "It's way too dark out here!"

Thomas the Pig said, "There is nothing to fear, Jesus is with you everywhere."

Wellington the Cow said with a fright, "I am afraid to go out at night."

Atarah the Tiger smiled and said, "Trust in Jesus, and you shall be led."

Wellington the Cow said, "What do you mean? How can I trust someone I have never seen?"

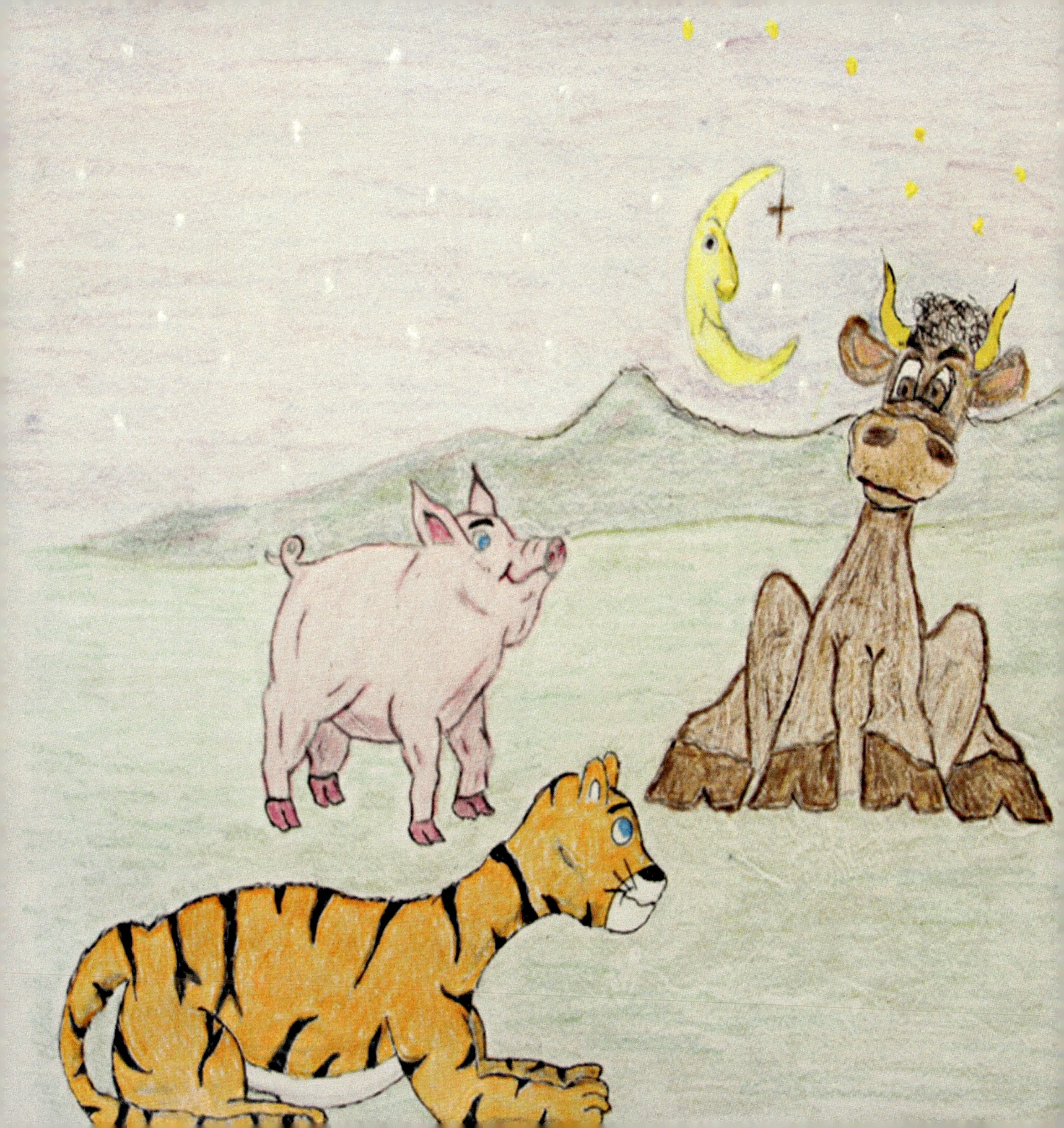

Hot Chocolate the Lioness answered, "Even though you don't see the Lord, He is there to lead you on forward.

Just believe in your heart that He is near saying out loud no fear, no fear, Jesus is here!"

"Yes, Yes" said Terrance the Horse "Jesus is the only way out of fear, of course."

Wellington the Cow amazed by what was said, decided to trust Jesus and be led.

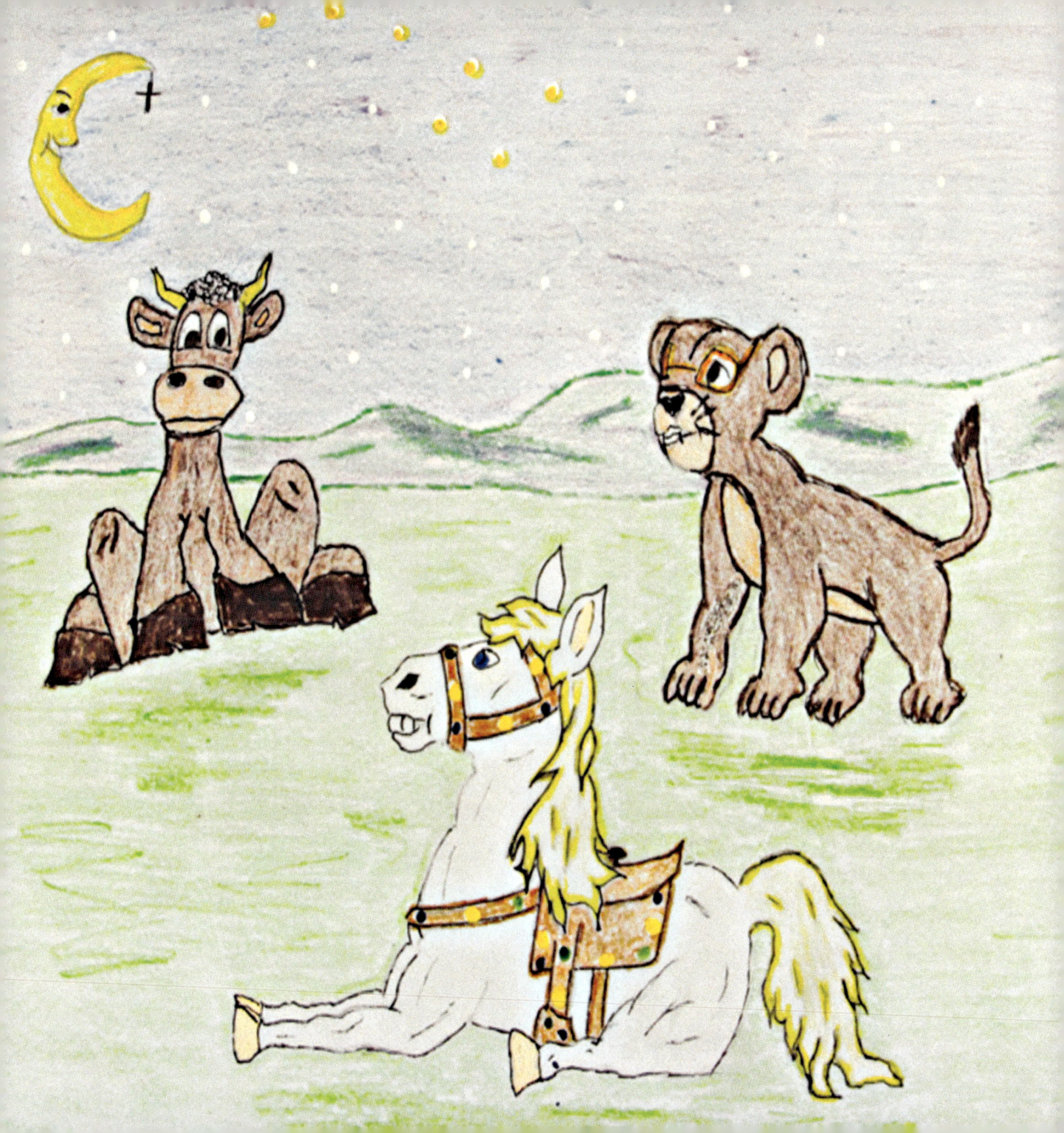

Deano the Eagle came down to say "Hi", because he seen them all together as he was soaring by.

They all gathered around Wellington the Cow all praising the Lord for what He did just now.

Saying "Thank you God for giving us your Son, to always be with us everywhere we go, thanks a ton!"

We learned how to get past our fears, by believing in our heart that Jesus is near. Saying out loud "No fear, no fear, Jesus is here!"

The End

Made in the USA
Monee, IL
14 April 2023